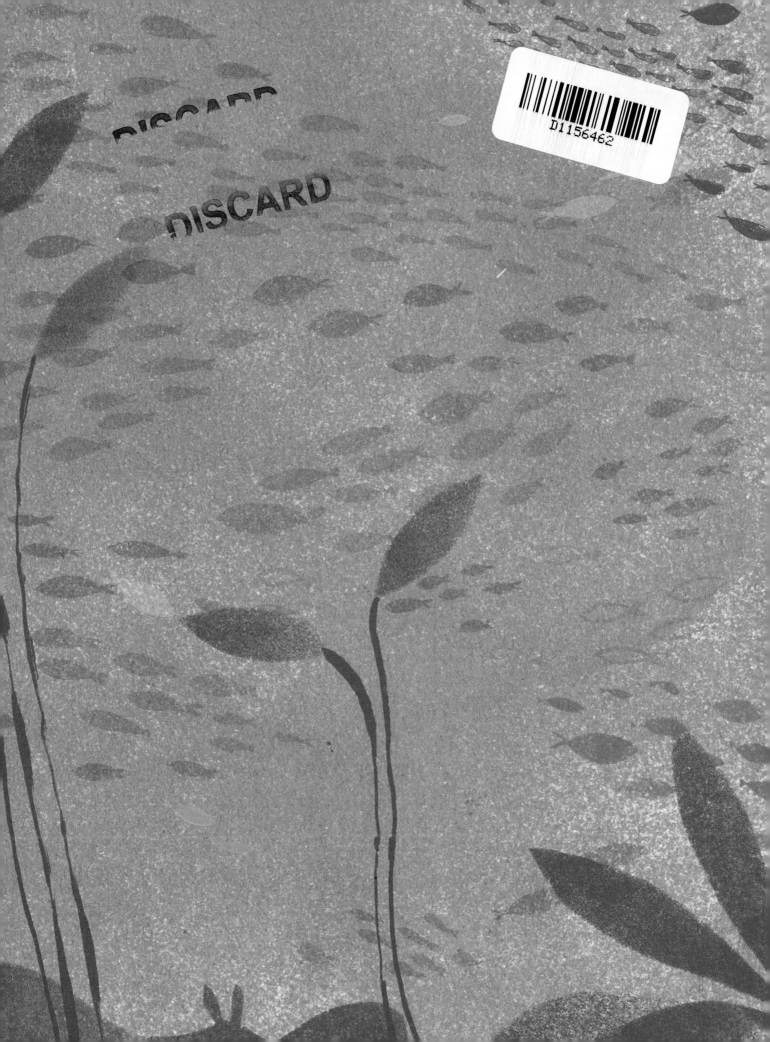

For Luka

First US edition 2021

Library of Congress Catalog Card Number pending
ISBN 978-1-5362-1531-1

CCP 10 9 8 7 6 5 4 3 2 1
26 25 24 23 22 21

Printed in Shenzhen, Guangdong, China

This book was typeset in Didact Gothic.
The illustrations were done in mixed media.

Candlewick Press
99 Dover Street
Somerville, Massachusetts 02144

www.candlewick.com

CANDLEWICK PRESS

THE WALLOOS'
BIG
ADVENTURE

ANUSKA ALLEPUZ

On a rocky island
beside a lake
lived the Walloo family:
Big Walloo,
Spotty Walloo,
Old Walloo,
and Little Walloo.

Little Walloo loved to tend to the tiny plants that sprouted up in between rocks.

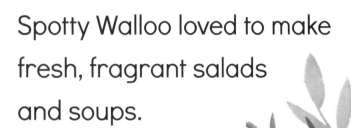

Spotty Walloo loved to make fresh, fragrant salads and soups.

Big Walloo loved to build things, especially boats.

And Old Walloo loved
to tell stories.

"In the old days," he said,
"I would visit tropical islands—
very BIG ones. You never saw
anything so beautiful!"

Little Walloo loved Old Walloo's stories.
How she wished to have her own adventure
and visit a tropical island!

Well, all Walloos love to go on trips . . .

so off they went in a brand-new boat built by Big Walloo.

For many days and many nights,
the Walloos sailed bravely across
the wide wild lake.
Until . . .

"LOOK! LOOK!
A tropical island!"
cried Little Walloo.
Her eyes grew wide.
Butterflies fluttered in her tummy.
"Wowee!"

The new island was beautiful and lush,
the air moist and fresh,
the plants tall and colorful.

But Little Walloo had a funny feeling,
almost as if the land was
rising and falling.

GURGLE!

WURGLE!

GURGLE!

But no one else noticed because there were so many things to do.

"I will build ten boats for each one of us!" cried Big Walloo.

"I will make the biggest and most delicious tropical Walloo cakes!" said Spotty Walloo.

Little Walloo and Old Walloo
loved wandering
the island together
and collecting seeds.

Over time, Little Walloo and Old Walloo
felt that the island was changing.
"Is the island . . . hotter?" asked Old Walloo.
"Is the island . . . moving?" asked Little Walloo.

They both agreed that
something wasn't right . . .

WURGLE!

GURGLE!

The land *was* moving!
Little Walloo bounced
and bounced
until she landed on . . .

a NOSE!

What is this?

Who is this?

"Hello! I'm Little Walloo.
I'm on a tropical island adventure
with my family!"

"Hello there, little one. I'm Hippo.
I was just about to dive
under the water.
It's far too hot for me
in this scorching sun."

"Where will you go?" asked Little Walloo.

"Where the plants are tall and colorful,
somewhere that will shelter me
from this burning heat," sighed Hippo.

The Walloos couldn't believe that
the tropical island was a HIPPO!
They looked around them and felt terrible.
Almost all the plants that had been
surrounding Hippo were gone.

"Please don't leave,"
cried Little Walloo.

She had an IDEA!

Everyone followed Little Walloo's brilliant plan.
Using the leaves they had taken,
Big Walloo and Spotty Walloo
built an umbrella for Hippo.

Hippo sighed deeply with happiness.

Meanwhile . . .

Little Walloo and Old Walloo spread the seeds
they had collected all around Hippo.

Soon, lots of plants started to grow
tall and colorful once more.

The air was moist
and fresh again.

Hippo began to feel
more like himself
as he enjoyed the
cool, sweet breeze.

Now Little Walloo had lots of stories to tell.
But these were stories that belonged
to them all—Hippo, too.

And with all the beautiful,
lush plants and delicious shade . . .

more and more hippos arrived!

And Little Walloo had many
more tropical adventures
with her Walloo family!